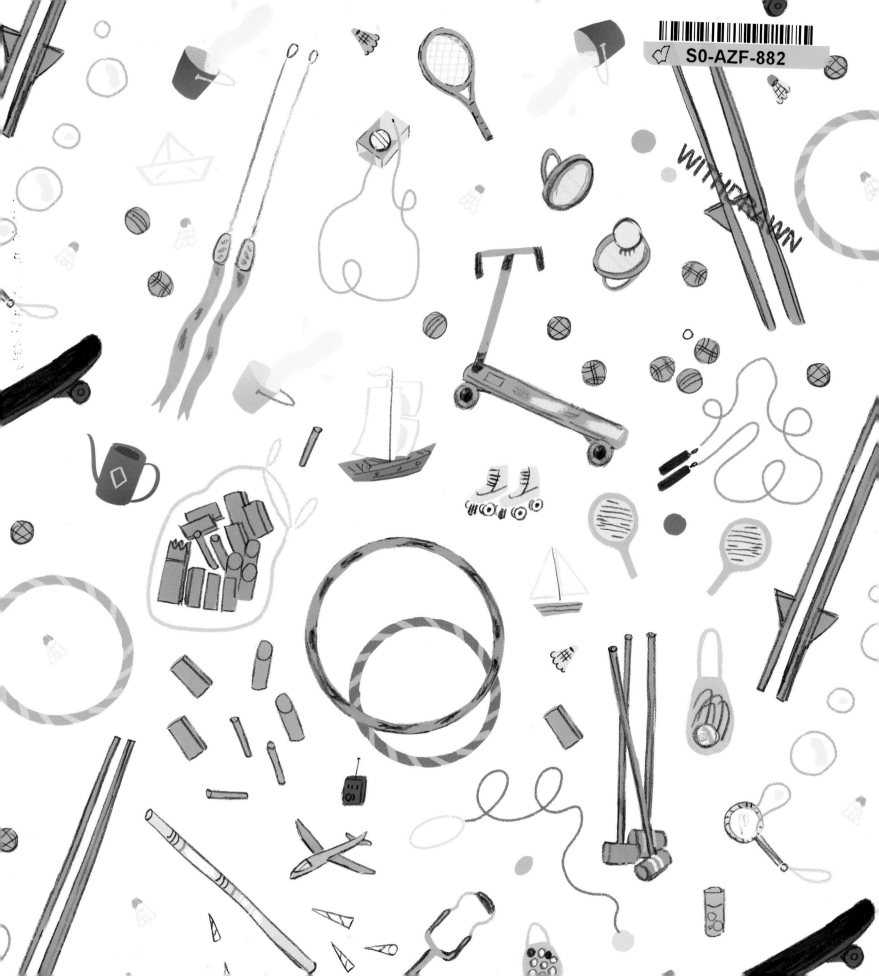

To my brother Michael.
– Adam Ciccio

A Beary Rainy Day written by Adam Ciccio and illustrated by Emilie Timmermans

ISBN 978-1-60537-598-4

This book was printed in January 2021 at Nikara, M. R. Štefánika 858/25, 963 01 Krupina, Slovakia.

First Edition
10 9 8 7 6 5 4 3 2 1

Written by Adam Ciccio

Illustrated by Emilie Timmermans

A BEARY RAINY DAY

Clavis
NEW YORK

Deep in the woods between the rocks and trees
where the leaves were green and yellow,
lived Wallow the Bear, unfortunately,
a quite gloomy fellow.

The funny thing was, and a tradition it became,
Wallow always got sad when it started to rain.
One morning, between the wooded pines and murky pond,
Wallow saw a rainstorm rolling along.

Wallow made plans to play outside,
but those feelings started to fizzle.
"I BETTER STAY IN TODAY,"
he said, as the rain started to drizzle.

From outside, Wallow moseyed right back around.
He shuffled back to his cozy bed.
He hunkered right back down.

Later that day, Wallow walked to the edge
of his cave to see about the rain.
Would Wallow be courageous and
go on an outdoorsy quest?

"NO," said Wallow, after seeing the owl
pouring buckets of water out of her nest.
**"I'M NOT GOING OUTSIDE!
THIS WEATHER IS BEING THE PESKIEST PEST."**

A few hours later, the rain fell harder on the forest floor.
Wallow wouldn't even make the walk to the edge
of the cave to check outside anymore.
That didn't stop Mother Nature, she rained harder than before.

So hard in fact, the rain leaked through
the cave and drip-dropped onto Wallow's head.
"I'VE HAD ENOUGH OF THIS!"
Wallow angrily said.
**"I'M SICK OF THIS RAIN.
I'M GOING BACK TO BED."**

Then, just as Wallow's eyes were about to close:

A NOISE...

AN ECHO...

It was his friend, Little Cub,
splashing in the puddles and laughing about.
"Hey, Wallow, I'm so happy you finally came out.
This is so much fun! You have to try it out!"

So Wallow and his friend splashed in the puddles as the hours went by.
Until the sun finally came out and the land got dry.

Wallow and his friend turned a gloomy day into fun,
and Wallow always played in the rain from that day on.

Wallow didn't get sad when it rained anymore.
He realized that gloominess wasn't because of the storm,

but because he'd never seen past the rain clouds before.

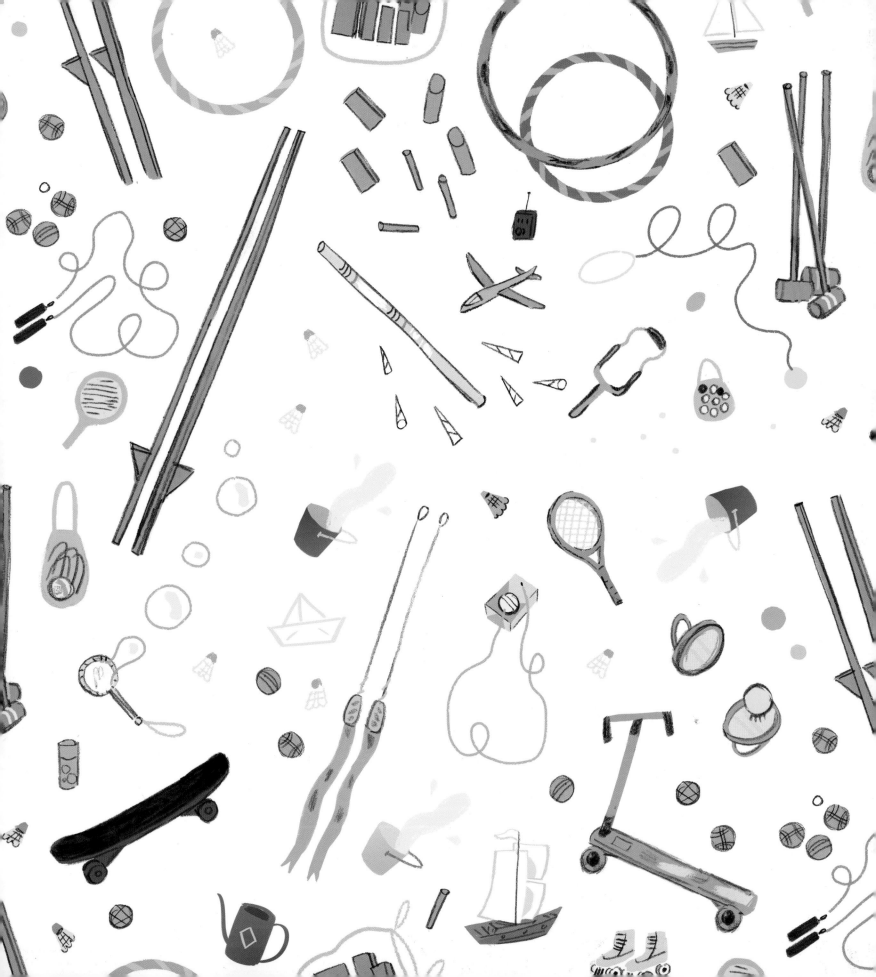